D1088582

Whatever Comes Tomorrow

WORDS BY Rebecca Gardyn Levington

ART BY Mariona Cabassa

Barefoot Books
step inside a story

Tomorrow
may bring endless sun
or swirly, snowy skies.

Tomorrow may bring new hellos
or difficult goodbyes.

Tomorrow
may bring loneliness
or laughter with a friend.
Tomorrow may bring words that wound
or ones that heal and mend.

Tomorrow
may bring changes
that are scary,
strange or new.

Tomorrow may bring chances
to embrace your truest you.

Tomorrow may bring obstacles
that seem too hard to face.

Tomorrow may bring feelings
that will need some extra space.

Tomorrow may bring questions that
you have no answers for...

3

. . . or answers that may lead you to
more questions than before.

Tomorrow may bring *anything*—

you have no way to know,

and sometimes that uncertainty
gives worries room to grow.

They sprout and bloom, consume your mind.
You want to run and hide.

But you've confronted fear before
and reached the other side.

You can't control
what happens next –
the what, the where, the how.

The only thing
in your control
is *you*.

Right here.
Right now.

You take a breath.

You close your eyes.

You whisper, “I am strong.”

You tell those worries in your head,
“I *know* I can. You're wrong.”

And when tomorrow disappears,
becoming yesterday,

you'll know for sure,
you *can* endure
whatever comes your way.

Tomorrow may bring laughter, love,
confusion, fear or fun,

an angry, rainy hurricane
or peaceful seaside sun.

Whatever comes tomorrow,
however steep the hill . . .

. . . you'll find your path.

You'll journey on.

You'll make it through.

You will.

Author's Note

Have you ever heard someone say that they have "butterflies" in their belly? It's a way to describe that fluttery feeling in your body whenever you start thinking about all the hard or scary things that *might* happen in the future. This feeling is called "worry" or "anxiety." Have you ever felt this way? If so, don't worry! Everyone feels anxious and has "butterflies" sometimes. (Did you notice all the butterflies in *this* book?)

When I was a kid, butterflies were constantly flying around inside my belly *and* my brain. Even as a grown-up, I still worry *a lot*. But I've learned that while I can't make the butterflies go away completely, there are techniques I can use to manage them so that they don't hold me back. (Check out the wonderful tips for managing worries described on this page. They really work!)

Whenever I feel extra overwhelmed by anxiety, two strategies work best for me. One is to remind myself of all the times I worried about something being "too hard" or "too scary" and, in the end, *I was wrong*. The other is to remind myself of all the times I worried and, in the end, *I was right*. Because, guess what? Sometimes things *were* super hard and scary. But even then, I *always* survived. I *always* pushed through. I am still here, and I will continue to brave *whatever* comes tomorrow.

And so, my friend, will you.

— Rebecca Gardyn Levington

Tips for Managing Worries

Written by Stefanie Paige Wieder, M.S.Ed., Child Development Specialist

Let's Get Started

- Can you think of a time you felt worried in a situation? What was going on?
- What did you feel in your body when you felt worried?
- What ended up happening?
- If you feel worried in that situation again, what could you say to that feeling? (For example, if you feel anxious about visiting a new place, you could say to that feeling: "I've never been here before, but I can ask a grown-up where things are if I am not sure.")

Calm Your Body

Often when we feel worried, our bodies tense up or we might even get a headache, stomachache or other body pain. This can feel very unpleasant. Here are some ways to calm your body until the anxious feeling passes:

- Squeeze playdough or a stress ball.
- Do some quick exercising like jumping jacks.
- Do a breathing technique like square breathing (see the next box).

Square Breathing

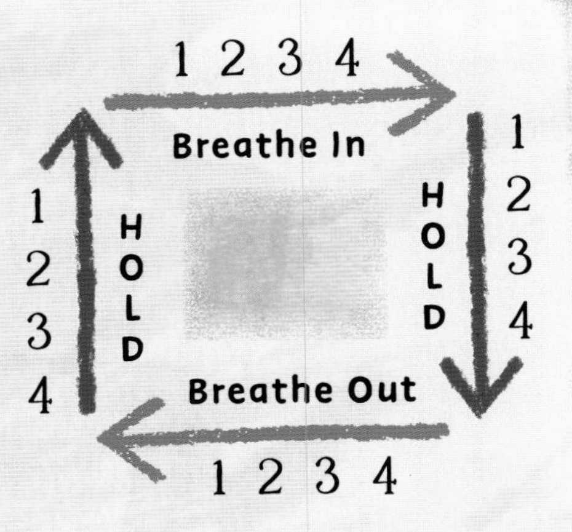

This kind of breathing can help you feel more relaxed. Sit or lie down and follow these steps:

1. Breathe in through your nose, counting to 4 slowly in your head.
2. Hold the breath in your lungs while you count to 4 again.
3. Breathe out through your mouth, slowly counting to 4 as you release the air.
4. Hold for a count of 4 before breathing in again.
5. Repeat steps 1 to 4 as many times as you like.

Make a Worry Plan

Write these prompts down on a piece of paper to make your own Worry Plan:

- The situation: ______________________ (Example: I'm worried my parent or caregiver won't pick me up on time.)
- I feel anxious about this when: ______________________ (Example: I'm at school.)
- A grown-up I can talk to about this feeling is: ______________________ (Examples: my teacher or my parent)
- Greet your feeling: "Hello, Anxiety. I see you."
- Something I can say to this feeling is: ______________________ (Example: They are usually on time. But if they are late, my teacher will stay with me until I get picked up.)
- Some things I can do to calm my body and mind until this feeling passes are: ______________________ (Examples: do square breathing or use my fidget toy)

Keep your Worry Plan in your pocket and pull it out next time you are in this situation. You can make a plan for any situation that makes you feel anxious.

Take a Break from Worries

Sometimes we wish we could take a break from anxious feelings. Here are some ideas for distracting yourself until the feelings pass:

- Read jokes or ask someone to tell you a joke.
- Play a game inside or outside, with a friend or on your own.
- Sing a song or dance to music.
- Play with a pet.
- Call someone you like to talk to.

For anyone whose worries sometimes feel too big to bear, remember:
tomorrow will soon be yesterday. Try to enjoy today. You've got this! – R. G. L.

To all the children who are growing up and learning to walk through life;
and to the inner child within every adult who is still exploring this journey. – M. C.

Illustrator's Note

It has been a challenge to draw sensations and emotions which can be difficult to describe, even if we have all – whether we are older or younger – experienced them throughout our lives. We might feel these "butterflies" inside us but not know how to name them or even what they look like!

Rebecca has done this with words in a very delicate and poetic way, while I have done my own exploration with the artwork. I interpreted some scenes as situations that children might experience every day, whereas for other scenes I have created something more abstract. I have tried with all of them to convey the same message that the text inspired in me: that all moments in life pass and change. We overcome them, we learn from them and we grow.

I wanted to include a lot of diversity and variety in all senses, through the characters, the shapes, the palette, the landscapes, so that – just like life – this book would have lots of movement and feel like a dance. I hope that readers young and old will be inspired to keep flying through this beautiful journey, with all its ups and downs. That is what life is!

– Mariona Cabassa

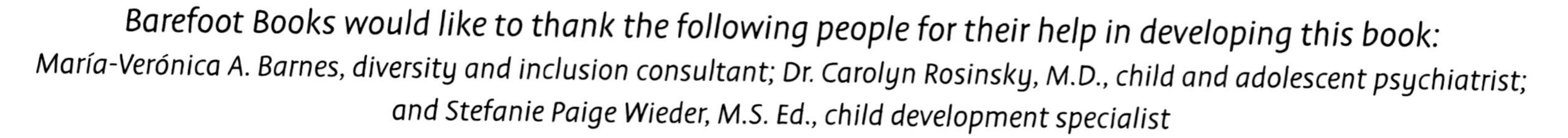

Barefoot Books would like to thank the following people for their help in developing this book:
María-Verónica A. Barnes, diversity and inclusion consultant; Dr. Carolyn Rosinsky, M.D., child and adolescent psychiatrist; and Stefanie Paige Wieder, M.S. Ed., child development specialist

Barefoot Books, 23 Bradford Street, 2nd Floor, Concord, MA 01742
Barefoot Books, 29/30 Fitzroy Square, London, W1T 6LQ

First published in the United States of America by Barefoot Books, Inc and in Great Britain by Barefoot Books, Ltd in 2023.

Graphic design by Sarah Soldano, Barefoot Books
Edited and art directed by Lisa Rosinsky, Barefoot Books

Reproduction by Bright Arts, Hong Kong. Printed in China
This book was typeset in Caprizant, Duper and Kidlit
The illustrations were prepared in crayons, gouache, pencils and water-based paints

Hardback ISBN 978-1-64686-841-4 | Paperback ISBN 978-1-64686-842-1
E-book ISBN 978-1-64686-859-9

British Cataloguing-in-Publication Data: a catalogue record for this book is available from the British Library

Library of Congress Cataloging-in-Publication data is available under LCCN 2022945116

1 3 5 7 9 8 6 4 2

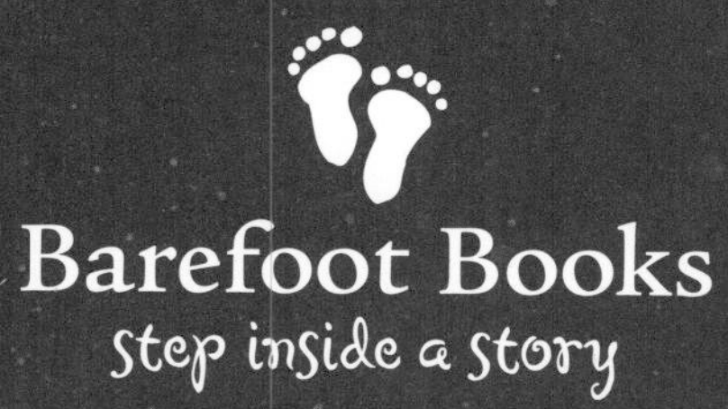

At Barefoot Books, we celebrate art and story that opens the hearts and minds of children from all walks of life, focusing on themes that encourage independence of spirit, enthusiasm for learning and respect for the world's diversity. The welfare of our children is dependent on the welfare of the planet, so we source paper from sustainably managed forests and constantly strive to reduce our environmental impact. Playful, beautiful and created to last a lifetime, our products combine the best of the present with the best of the past to educate our children as the caretakers of tomorrow.

www.barefootbooks.com

Rebecca Gardyn Levington

is a children's book author, poet and journalist with a particular penchant for penning both playful and poignant picture books and poems – primarily in rhyme. Rebecca's award-winning poems and articles have appeared in numerous anthologies, newspapers and magazines. She lives in the suburban jungles of New Jersey, USA, with her husband and two boisterous boys. *RebeccaGardynLevington.com*

Mariona Cabassa

is a native of Catalonia, Spain, and has illustrated over 80 children's books. She studied at art school in Barcelona, followed by further research in Strasbourg, France. Her many subsequent years of working as an illustrator, painter, installation maker and tattoo artist reflect her fascination with form and her desire to explore different palettes. Mariona's technique combines water-based paints, pencils and a digital touch to create rich and detailed illustrations. *TheInvisibleCircle.com*